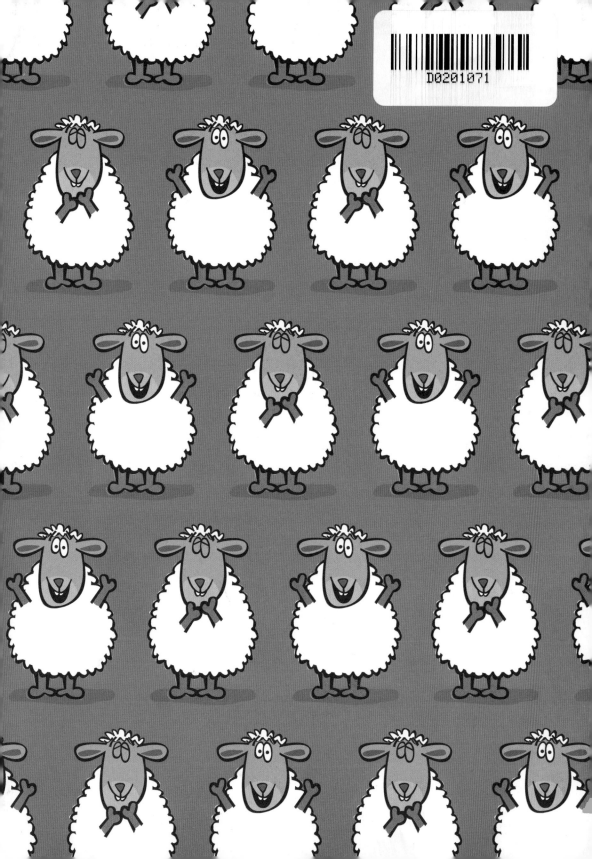

For ET

The illustrations in this book were done digitally.
The text type was set in Chaloops and Eatwell Chubby.
The display type was set in Eatwell Chubby.

ISBN 978-0-544-96655-0

Manufactured in China
SCP 10 9 8 7 6 5 4 3
4500700827

My Friends Make Me HAPPY!

JAN THOMAS

Yay!
Look who's coming!
My FRIENDS!

Houghton Mifflin Harcourt

Boston   New York

But, after **us**,
what makes
you **HAPPY**,
Sheep?

Looking for more laughs?

There's a **PEST** in the Garden!
JAN THOMAS

My Toothbrush Is **MISSING**
JAN THOMAS

What Is Chasing Duck?
JAN THOMAS

Get your child ready to read in three simple steps!

1 I READ	Read the book to your child.
2 WE READ	Read the book together.
3 YOU READ	Encourage your child ... { over and over again.